Ladybird books are widely available, but in case of
difficulty may be ordered by post or telephone from:

Ladybird Books – Cash Sales Department
Littlegate Road Paignton Devon TQ3 3BE
Telephone 0803 554761

A catalogue record for this book is available
from the British Library

Published by Ladybird Books Ltd Loughborough Leicestershire UK
Ladybird Books Inc Auburn Maine 04210 USA

Printed in EC

DESPERATE DAN

DIAMOND DISASTER

Ladybird

Desperate Dan likes nothing better than to start the day with a large, crusty cow-pie for breakfast and then perhaps one or two after that to help it down. But this morning he was eating more cow-pies than usual.

"Thanks, Aunt Aggie!" said Desperate Dan after he had scoffed the lot, for Aggie was the only person in the world who knew the secret recipe for Dan's cow-pie.

Dan reckoned it was time he showed his appreciation to Aunt Aggie for all the cow-pies she'd made for him over the years.

"This ought to do me," he said, as he emptied his life savings out of a metal rhinoceros bank – piggy banks were MUCH too soft for Dan!

Then he marched down to the Cactusville Jewellers. He knew that Aggie had always wanted a beautiful, shiny diamond ring. Unfortunately, the rings there were very expensive!

"And ah've only got fifty cents," sighed Dan.

Aunt Aggie deserved the best. But what could Dan do?

"Ah've got it!" he said. "Ah'm gonna look for diamonds out in the hills!"

So Dan went to buy his diamond-hunting gear from the general store. "You'll need a shovel, a pickaxe, dynamite, a mule, food, a stove, a torch, a map, a diamond spotter's book – and you're gonna want some sweet tea as well!" advised the storekeeper.

"Why's that?" asked Dan.

"For the shock, in case you DO find a diamond!"

Soon Dan had loaded all the supplies onto his mule.

"There you go, little feller!" he said. But the poor thing couldn't take all the weight, and Dan did hate to see it suffer.

"This won't do at all, pardner!" said Dan, and before long the supplies were well on their way to the hills, with Dan carrying them AND the mule on his back!

"You okay back there?" he asked. The mule grunted happily. This DID make a change for him!

When Dan got to the hills, he laid out his equipment.

"Let's see now," he said. "These rocks look promisin'!" And with that he whacked at them with his pickaxe to see if there were diamonds inside.

Meanwhile, two whole miles away there was chaos at the fort of the 7th Cavalry Troopers.

"Man your posts, everyone!" screamed the panicked General Cactushead. "We're under attack!"

They weren't, of course. The stones raining down on them were the chippings from Dan's rocks!

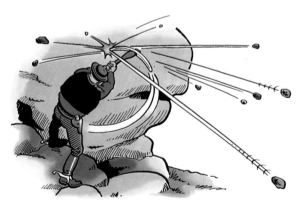

"How about in here?" wondered Dan, standing at the entrance of a likely cave. "It's probably an old, abandoned diamond mine. There's sure to be diamonds in there!"

Dan entered the cave and saw something shining just ahead.

"Well, what did I say?" said Dan, excited by his find. "I've struck gold— I mean, diamonds! Aunt Aggie's gonna love her diamond ring!"

But things weren't quite what they seemed.

A deafening 'THUD!' echoed round the whole cave, then Desperate Dan stumbled out. "Huh! No diamonds after all."

Following Dan out of the cave was the Texas express, chugging along as best it could after crashing into Dan. Dan had mistaken the railway tunnel for a cave – and the lights that he'd seen were the lights of the train!

But Dan was more determined than ever to find a dazzling diamond for Aunt Aggie.

"Maybe ah'll have more luck at the base of this mountain," said Dan, digging more and more furiously.

"Hoo-ee! This sure is hard work," he groaned, but he mopped his brow and carried on digging.

"Well, I'll be darned," said Dan when he stopped and saw what had happened. The big galoot had dug so hard that he'd moved the mountain half a mile east!

"Darn nuisance, that's all I can say!" grumbled the owner of the Mountain View Hotel. Because there was no longer a mountain to view he'd have to think of a new name for the hotel.

The pony express rider also had reason to grumble.

"Whew! Where'd this great thing come from?" he gasped as Dan's new mountain towered above him. "It's totally blocking my trail! I'm gonna need a mountain goat to get over that tower of rubble!"

But Dan didn't stop there. He carried right on, until...

"Darn tootin'! I've got one! I've actually found one of the perishers!"

Dan jumped for joy at his discovery. "This just has to be the biggest rootin' diamond I've ever seen!"

But it was a little bit grubby, so Dan polished it on his chin. "Yup, I'll get this dazzler as good as new in no time!"

But, as Dan rubbed the stone, bits of the diamond fell away like grains of salt until there was nothing left but a pile of dust. A diamond may be the hardest thing around, but it just couldn't handle the stubble on Dan's chin.

Dan was furious! "Sufferin' gemstones! I had it right there in mah mitts – and now it's gone again!" he bellowed.

All the rabbits for miles around shot out of their burrows. They thought the commotion was an earthquake!

CRUMBLE!

Dan was downright depressed. When he got home, Aunt Aggie landed a loving, soggy kiss on his cheek.

"Jeepers, Aunt Aggie!" said Dan. "What's come over you?"

"Your face, of course!" The diamond had shaved Dan clean for the first time since he was two weeks old. "How thoughtful of you! Finally I can kiss my favourite nephew without scratching my face!"

Boy, did Dan blush! He thought he didn't have anything to thank Aggie with, but he'd actually given her what she'd always wanted. What a close shave!